LIBRARY OF AWESOME ANIMALS

ORCA

By Rachel Rose

Consultant: Darin Collins, DVM
Director, Animal Health Programs, Woodland Park Zoo

BEARPORT
PUBLISHING

Minneapolis, Minnesota

Credits

cover, © Tory Kallman/Shutterstock; 3, © Musat/iStock; 4, 5, © Nature Picture Library/Alamy Stock Photo; 6, © slowmotiongli/Shutterstock; 7, © Tory Kallman/Shutterstock; 9, © Graeme Snow/Shutterstock; 10, 11, © Tory Kallman/Shutterstock; 11, © Lazareva/iStock; 13, © Arco Images GmbH/Alamy Stock Photo; 15, © slowmotiongli/Shutterstock; 17, © Foto 4440/Shutterstock; 18, © Rich Carey/Shutterstock; 19, © Thanaphong Araveeporn/Shutterstock; 21, © slowmotiongli/Shutterstock; 23, © Alexander Baumann/Shutterstock

President: Jen Jenson
Director of Product Development: Spencer Brinker
Editor: Allison Juda
Designer: Micah Edel

Library of Congress Cataloging-in-Publication Data

Names: Rose, Rachel, 1968- author.
Title: Orca / Rachel Rose.
Description: Minneapolis : Bearport Publishing Company, [2021] | Series: Library of awesome animals | Includes bibliographical references and index.
Identifiers: LCCN 2020008971 (print) | LCCN 2020008972 (ebook) | ISBN 9781647471477 (library binding) | ISBN 9781647471583 (paperback) | ISBN 9781647471699 (ebook)
Subjects: LCSH: Killer whale—Juvenile literature.
Classification: LCC QL737.C432 R67 2021 (print) | LCC QL737.C432 (ebook) | DDC 599.53—dc23
LC record available at https://lccn.loc.gov/2020008971
LC ebook record available at https://lccn.loc.gov/2020008972

Copyright © 2021 Bearport Publishing Company. All rights reserved. No part of this publication may be reproduced in whole or in part, stored in any retrieval system, or transmitted in any form or by any means, electronic, mechanical, photocopying, recording, or otherwise, without written permission from the publisher.

For more information, write to Bearport Publishing, 5357 Penn Avenue South, Minneapolis, MN 55419. Printed in the United States of America.

Contents

Awesome Orcas! 4
Big and Beautiful 6
Take a Deep Breath 8
Family Ties 10
Cute Calf 12
Top of the Class 14
What's for Dinner? 16
Watch Out! 18
Born to Be Wild 20

Information Station 22
Glossary 23
Index 24
Read More 24
Learn More Online 24
About the Author 24

AWESOME Orcas!

SPLASH! An orca leaps out of the water. With a huge black-and-white body flying through the air, the orca is awesome!

A FULLY GROWN ORCA CAN WEIGH AS MUCH AS TWO ELEPHANTS.

Big and Beautiful

Orcas are often called killer whales. But orcas aren't whales at all. They're dolphins!

Everything about this dolphin is big. It has a huge fin, big **flippers**, and a giant tail. Even orca teeth are big. Each tooth is about 4 inches (10.1 cm) long.

THE MALE ORCA'S FIN CAN GROW UP TO 6 FEET (1.8 M) TALL.

Take a Deep Breath

Orcas live in the ocean, but they cannot breathe under water. They need to come to the surface to breathe at least every 15 minutes. Unlike humans, orcas need to think about breathing. Because of this, only half of the orca's brain can sleep at a time. Otherwise, they would not go to the surface to breathe and would die without air. **WOW!**

ORCAS ONLY CLOSE ONE EYE WHEN THEY SLEEP. THE EYE CONNECTED TO THE HALF OF THE BRAIN THAT IS AWAKE STAYS OPEN.

An orca breathes through a blowhole.

Family Ties

Orcas travel through all of the world's oceans in family groups called **pods**. Each pod has its own **diet**. The orcas in each pod also have their own way of speaking to one another. Their calls keep the family group connected over long distances.

THERE CAN BE UP TO 40 ORCAS IN A POD. PODS ARE LED BY FEMALE ORCAS.

Cute Calf

Pods grow as female orcas have babies. They can start to do this when they are about 15 years old. After **mating**, it can take 17 months for a baby orca to grow inside its mother. A baby orca is called a calf.

As soon as a calf is born, it swims to the surface of the water to take its first breath. The calf drinks its mother's milk for about two years. *SLURP!*

A YOUNG CALF DRINKS MILK FROM ITS MOTHER'S BODY. OFTEN, THE PAIR KEEPS MOVING WHILE THE CALF IS FEEDING.

Top of the Class

Did you know orcas are some of the smartest animals on Earth? Orcas are quick learners. They have good memories. They are very good at working in groups and solving problems. The way orcas **communicate**—through calls, clicks, and whistles—also shows how smart they are. That's awesome!

AN ORCA'S BRAIN WEIGHS UP TO 15 POUNDS (6.8 KG).

15

What's for Dinner?

Orcas communicate when they hunt in groups. And that's good. Because they eat *a lot*—up to 500 lb (226.8 kg) of food in a single day! They will snap up fish, seals, sea lions, penguins, and even whales.

Orcas have many different ways to catch their **prey**. In cold waters, orcas make waves to knock a penguin or sea lion off floating ice and into the water. Sometimes, orcas even jump onto land to snatch a meal or scare a seal into the water. *CHOMP!*

ORCAS DON'T CHEW THEIR FOOD. THEY CAN SWALLOW A SMALL SEA LION WHOLE!

Watch Out!

Orcas are so big and strong that they have no natural **predators**. However, humans are a **threat** to orcas. Even though it is banned, people still kill orcas for their meat and oil. **Pollution** in the oceans is also harmful to orcas.

Sometimes, orcas are captured and brought to animal parks and **aquariums**. This is bad for the animals.

ORCAS TAKEN OUT OF THE OCEAN DO NOT HAVE ENOUGH SPACE TO MOVE. WHEN THIS HAPPENS, THEY GET BORED AND STRESSED.

Born to Be Wild

When they are left in the wild, orcas can live long and active lives. They spend their days swimming through the ocean. Orcas travel about 40 miles (74 km) every day! They can dive up to 500 ft (152.4 m) below water.

Orcas are some of the smartest and most powerful creatures in the ocean. They are awesome!

IN THE WILD, MALE ORCAS LIVE FOR UP TO 60 YEARS. FEMALES SOMETIMES LIVE UP TO 90 YEARS!

Information Station

ORCAS ARE AWESOME!
LET'S LEARN EVEN MORE ABOUT THEM.

Kind of animal: Like all dolphins, orcas are mammals. Mammals are warm-blooded animals whose young drink milk. Orcas are different from other mammals because they don't have fur.

Other dolphins: Orcas are 1 of 36 kinds of dolphins found in the ocean's waters.

Size: Orcas are 23–32 ft (7–9.8 m) long. That's almost as long as a school bus!

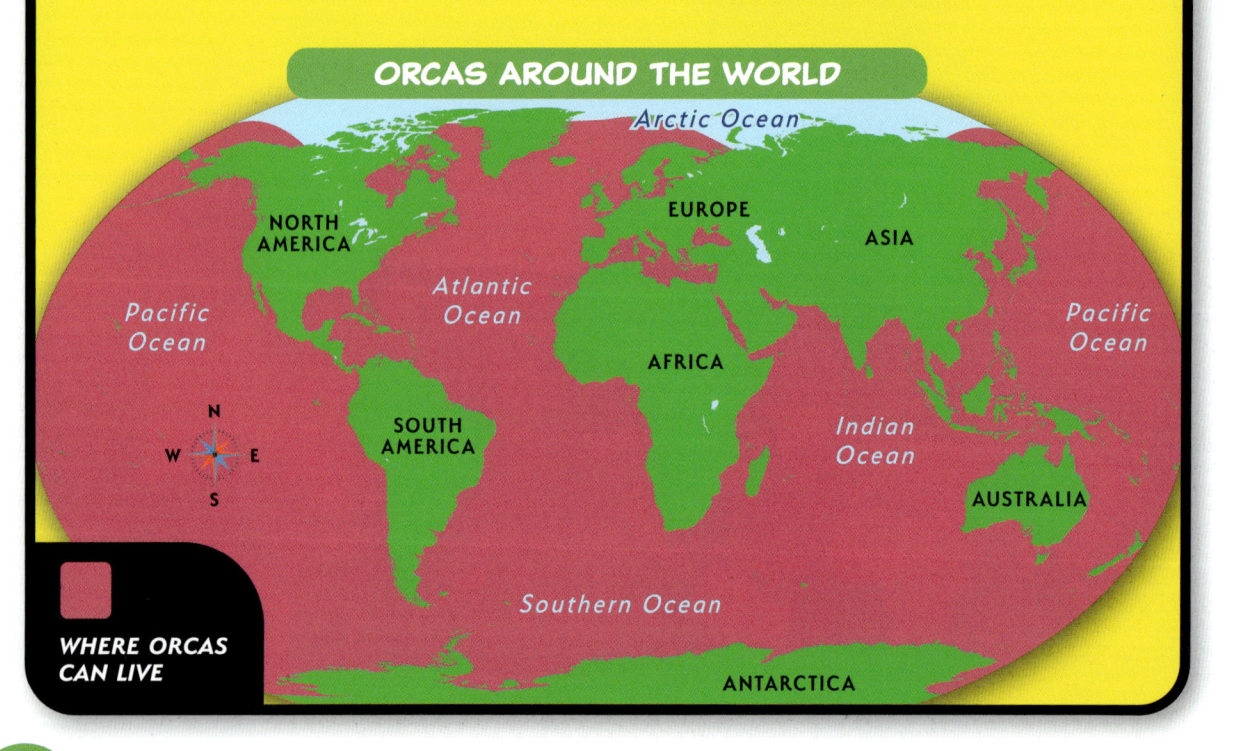

ORCAS AROUND THE WORLD

Arctic Ocean
NORTH AMERICA
EUROPE
ASIA
Pacific Ocean
Atlantic Ocean
AFRICA
Pacific Ocean
SOUTH AMERICA
Indian Ocean
AUSTRALIA
Southern Ocean
ANTARCTICA

WHERE ORCAS CAN LIVE

Glossary

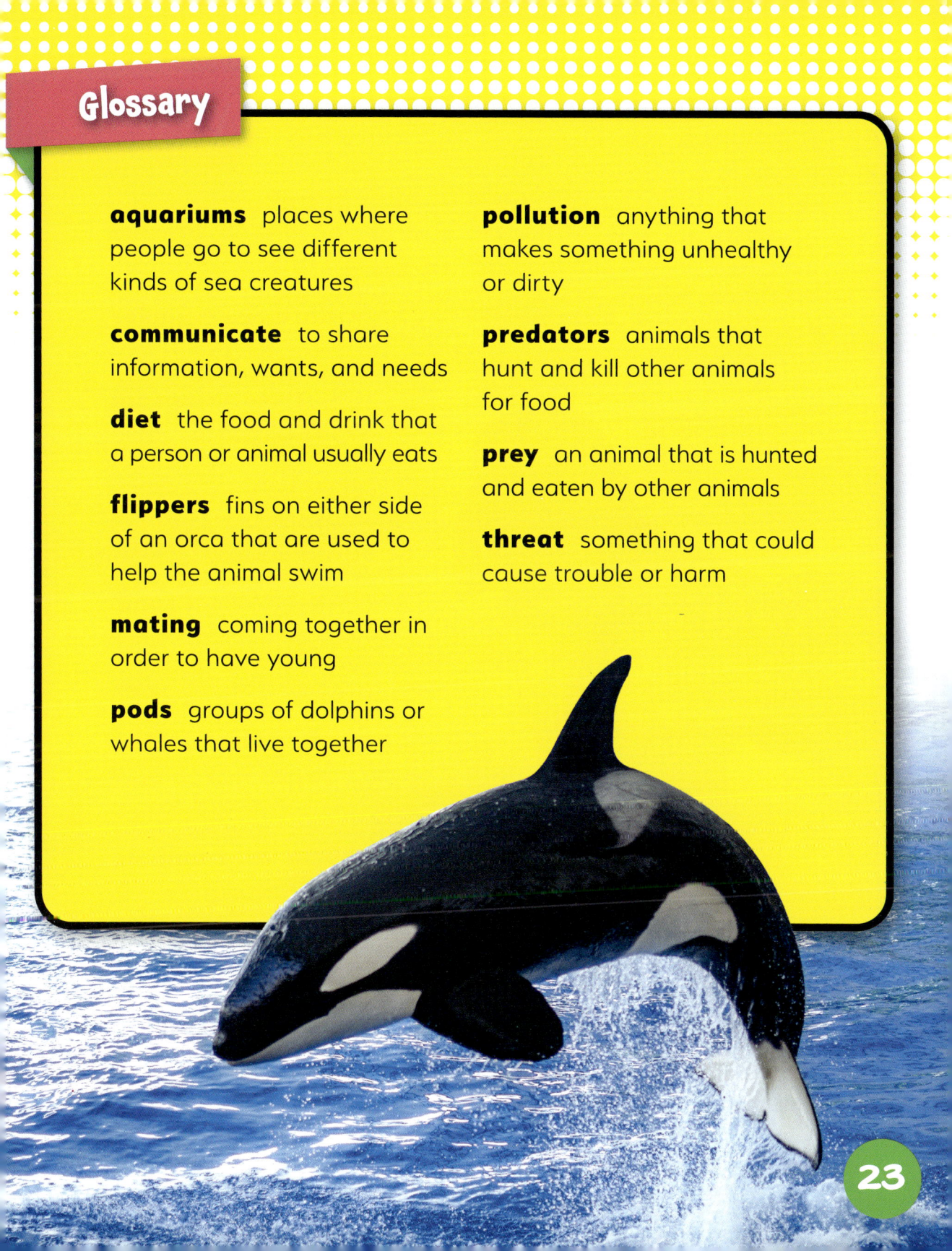

aquariums places where people go to see different kinds of sea creatures

communicate to share information, wants, and needs

diet the food and drink that a person or animal usually eats

flippers fins on either side of an orca that are used to help the animal swim

mating coming together in order to have young

pods groups of dolphins or whales that live together

pollution anything that makes something unhealthy or dirty

predators animals that hunt and kill other animals for food

prey an animal that is hunted and eaten by other animals

threat something that could cause trouble or harm

Index

brains 8–9, 14
breathing 8–9, 12
calf 12–13
communication 14, 16
dolphins 6
food 16–17
humans 8, 18
hunting 16
penguin 16
pods 10–12
sea lions 16–17
seals 16
teeth 6
threats 18
whale 6, 16

Read More

Adamson, Heather. *Orcas (Blastoff! Readers. Ocean Life Up Close)*. Minneapolis: Bellwether Media (2018).

Krajnik, Elizabeth. *Orcas (Killers of the Animal Kingdom)*. New York: PowerKids Press (2020).

Learn More Online

1. Go to **www.factsurfer.com**
2. Enter "**Orca**" into the search box.
3. Click on the cover of this book to see a list of websites.

About the Author

Rachel Rose writes books for children and teaches yoga. She lives in San Francisco with her husband and her dog, Sandy.